Gifts of the Heart

by Karen Boes Oman

illustrated by Marilyn Brown

"*Finally*, we're here!"
Grandpa said, "What a day!
Grandchildren, our story
will whisk you away."

"So, go give your Grandma
a kiss and a hug.
Then come and sit by me
like bugs on a rug."

$\mathcal{T}$his morning I said,

"**Christmas Eve is today.**"

Grandma cheered, "Time to

visit our grandkids and play!"

We packed up your presents,

from out of the drawers,

from under the beds
and from hooks behind the doors.

There were warm woolen coats,
red boots and red socks,
eight shiny skates,
and a toy horse that rocks!

The weatherman **promised** blue skies for the day,
but a **terrible snowstorm** surprised us halfway.
The wind picked our car up and twirled us around.
It blew open our car door — **your gifts it had found!**

It blew them and threw them, and off they all flew.
When it stopped, our car dropped, and it plopped on a shoe!

Your coats,
just like ornaments,
dressed up a **tree**,
and the kids from the shoe squealed,
"This one's for me!"

HAPPY
KIDS
HOME

"Our coats!"
I whispered into
Grandma's ear.
She whispered back,
"**Dear**, they'll be
warming kids **here**."

"For I see a need, and so if I start
giving coats to the coatless, I'm giving my heart."

$\mathcal{S}$woop! Socks and boots flew right over my head,

and I called out to Grandma, "Let's chase these instead!"

Our gifts found the cottage of Little Bo Peep,

who was weeping, "The snowstorm has hidden my sheep!"

Then to our surprise, came
"Bleat! Bleat! Bleat! Bleat!"
and the red socks and boots
were now on her sheep's feet!

I thought, "That's a need, and so if I start
giving boots to the bootless, I'm giving my heart."

Bo Peep was so merry!
We rode in her sleigh,
zipping up, skipping down,
and we laughed the whole way.

Grandma gave me that look:
I thought, "Not the **skates** too!"
But we left the big spider
the skates meant
for you.

'Til I
spotted a spider
who made figure eights,
and I hollered, "Hey spider!
You're wearing our skates!"

The winds seemed to whisper,
"Whenever you start
giving skates to the skateless,
you're **giving your
heart**."

*W*hoosh! The wind pushed Grandma up in the sky,

and she yelled down to me, "Flap your arms and you'll fly."

We sailed past the ice rink, Bo Peep's, and the shoe.

We flew and we flew 'til we came home to you.

Grandpa paused in his story.
Then one child tapped his knee,
"Where'd the rocking horse go?
Is it stuck in a tree?"

Grandpa sighed sadly,
"Your rocking horse crashed.
Grandma picked up his tail,
but your last gift was smashed."

The kids hugged their Grandpa,
"No gifts, that's okay.
By next year we'd think
they were old anyway."

Rap! Rap! Rap! Rap!
Guess who stood at their door?
'Twas Bo Peep with her sheep
and their red feet galore.

"Could each of you kindly step into my sleigh?

Your car's off the shoe, but that's all I can say!

And grandkids," she added, "Please buckle up tight.

I'm in a big rush, so we're flying tonight!"

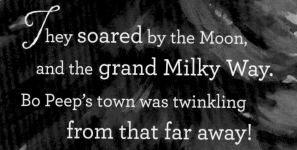

They soared by the Moon,
and the grand Milky Way.
Bo Peep's town was twinkling
from that far away!

And as they drew closer, folks bustled about
in shops dressed for Christmas, both inside and out.

Bo Peep's flying fleet floated over a tower
and touched down below as its clock struck the hour.

She waved her staff once, and all stood amazed
as the Christmas tree magically sparkled and blazed.
She waved her staff twice, and bells started ringing,
and three times gave everyone beautiful singing.

"Grandkids, there's more!" sang out Little Bo Peep.
"My sheep knit you beanies and blankies to keep.
The spider has spun you a net just for fun,
and his friend brought you tuffets to rest when you're done."

"The kids from the shoe made you dolls from their tree.
And," Little Bo Peep cried, "just wait 'til you see!"

"Your toy rocking horse which had crashed on the trail?"
The town cheered, "We glued it, except for its tail!"

Grandma said to the townsfolk, "We'll never forget
these gifts of the heart: they're the best presents yet!
When you see a need, and then if you start,
to give what is needed, you're giving your heart."

They thanked their new friends
as they packed up to go.
Grandma, Grandpa, and grandkids
drove home through the snow.

And everyone knew
that the best gift that night
was learning that giving
makes hearts feel just right.

The End